The Buckleys

Ben Robinson III

ISBN:1517585600
ISBN-13:9781517585600

DEDICATION

This book is dedicated to my parents Benny and Gladys, because their belief in me has always been the voice that propels me to never give up. Through them I am the man that I am, and every success and accomplishment I acquire in my life is for them.

ACKNOWLEDGMENTS

I want to take this opportunity to Thank everyone who has ever told me to just do it. This is the first of many books and it is through your encouragement and faith that I will continue to make my dreams a reality.

Mr. and Mrs. Joseph William Buckley

Along with

Ms. Constance McGill-Cassidy

Cordially Invite You to the Union of Their Children

Brendan Alexander Buckley and ***Gloria Chase Cassidy***   .

Saturday February 15

Cathedral of the Holy Cross

Boston Massachusetts

3PM

The Rehearsal Dinner

Sometimes when I look at my family I can only find two words to describe them.

Fucking. **Assholes**.

First you got Carlene; the tiny, neurotic, cosmetically enhanced science-fiction project who actually grew up in Southie but has made a career of keeping that a secret from all of her fellow Beacon Hill fair-weather friends.

The ironic thing is that most of those broads are from Roxbury, and nowhere near the good part either.

And then there's Joe, the retired Army vet with a gun in every room of our house, who once referred to an Iranian pizza delivery man as "*the enemy come a 'knockin*".

Yes, *those* are my parents.

"Jeffrey..." My mother called out to me while clutching a half empty glass of Pinot Grigio. I think it was her eighth or ninth glass of the night. Honestly, I learned to stop counting the number of drinks she could consume because she has a sponge liver that never needs to be wrung out. I remember, at my oldest brother Gene's college graduation barbecue, I clocked her at 20 glasses of Riesling and she still was sober enough to volunteer to drive to Shaw's for more wine.

"Where is Brendan?" She slurred.

"I think him and Scootie just ran out for some more beer." I answered her, and panic flashed across her face before she pulled out her iPhone, which was imprisoned inside of a sparkly pink case.

God Mom, what are you? Twelve?

"Brendan...it's Mom......." she spoke into the receiver with enough volume to drown out the DJ's set of cheesy Top 40 hits. "No, not Maude...MOM......Brendan....it's your mother..." I chuckled to myself thinking how pathetic she looked. She squinted in disgust as she shot her eyes between the annoying DJ and me.

God this music sucks. If he plays that Ke$ha song one more time *he's* gonna die young when I throw my mother's stupid iPhone into the middle of his forehead David and Goliath style.

"Yeah, get more wine...." she continued. "...WINE.....W-I-N.......What? No, not weed, WINE.....But wait, get some weed if you can." She paused. "WEED"

As I watched her I could see that she had forgotten I was standing there, so she walked away from me to continue trying to score drugs from her son.

It was a quarter past eleven and everyone was still drinking and carrying on as if Chase and Brendan's wedding wasn't taking place the next day. Chase's hot younger sisters Donna and Christy were continuing their drunken flirtation with a few of Brendan's equally drunk frat brothers while Chase was doing body shots with her *hotter* girl cousins from Miami at a bar in a darkened corner of the banquet hall.

How can I describe Gloria Chase Cassidy in one word?

Honestly, that's really hard to do. As far as I can remember she's always been the "fun" girl. She could easily drink beer and watch baseball with the guys, but not in a manly way where she's trying to be like them. Chase always put out the "Yeah, you can fuck me like a porn star after everyone leaves" kind of vibe. And she was no stranger to being seen as one of *those* types of girls, but Chase never gave a shit about what other people think.

I guess when you're born into a prominent family and grow up to be the pretty girl you can do whatever you want.

"Jeffrey" my mom approached me again after ending her phone call with my idiot brother. "Go find your father and tell him I'm going home."

"What about the wine?"

She cringed then laughed. "Brendan said he'll meet me at home with it. No need in supplying these people with anymore free alcohol."

As she finished her sentence Scootie's parents Dr. and Mrs. McBride approached her with some more warm words about Brendan and his upcoming nuptials. Their accolades thrust Mom back into Proud Mother Mode for the thousandth time that evening. Just like she'd always done whenever it came to Brendan she began doting on him, allowing the Botox to work overtime by giving the smoothness in her face an opportunity to not crack as she smiled. I've seen old pictures of Mom back in the day and she was pretty hot before all of the plastic surgery. But mentally, she's still stuck at twentyfive when she was a mother to two small boys and could still see the face God gave her whenever she looked into a mirror. I have no idea how a slope headed curmudgeon like my dad ended up with such a hot wife. She was either attracted to his personality or knocked up at the time and forced to marry him by my strict Catholic grandparents.

I'm banking on the latter.

I left Mom to her Oscar-worthy performance with the McBride's to look for anyone other than her to be around. I love her, but in social situations she becomes a little too much to handle.

I noticed the crowd thinning out in the main hall and it was quite a sight too. There were so many pasty, pale, balding white men and their overly made-up wives gathering designer purses, lengthy fur coats and other accessories which basically screams to onlookers *"We've made it! Look at all of our pretty things!"*

But I'm not stupid. I know that we grew up wealthy. I realize that in the greater scheme of things our families have known privilege that others can only dream of. But I also realize that everything in life has a cost. And the cost of all this opulence lies in the broken families we hail from and the disconnect we as kids have from our parents.

As I looked across the room through the crowd of deserters I noticed Brendan's Best Man Scootie chatting up one of Chase's homelier bridesmaids. That was when I realized Brendan wasn't with him, which made me *really* wonder where he had snuck off to.

Scootie was a hometown hero in Boston but all I ever saw was a huge, unconscionable douche bag. Him and Brendan were the nerdy fat kids when they were younger but thanks to our fathers they developed a love for football at an early age and slimmed down to play during high school. Brendan stopped playing by the time he got to college, but Scootie continued on as a Wide Receiver at Boston University.

Whenever I stop to think about it I still can't believe that he plays for the New York Giants but Scootie is a beast on the field, so I can't be mad at his success.

Still, the worst thing you can do for someone who's always been insecure is give them a taste of fame.

Because Scootie's a fucking asshole too.

"JEFF-FAYYYYY!!!!" He bellowed, his deep voice tipsy but still bro-like. He put his arm around me and I smiled, noticing his Super Bowl ring sparkle like fireworks on his finger. I love Scootie because I grew up with him but I could never vouch for his character.

He's always made his home in Brendan's shadow.
"Yo, that girl's hot ain't she?" He asked, and I knew he was drunk because the girl he was pointing to looked like a wildebeest in drag. Had she not come from a family of hot chicks she wouldn't even be allowed to throw rice at the wedding, let alone be in it.

I wanted to tell him to take her out back and fuck her behind the dumpster but before I could Chase appeared. She placed her hand on my shoulder to keep her balance while laughing.

"Are you trying to fuck my cousin Whitney?" She asked him. Scootie stared in silence because he was caught off guard when Chase popped up, but the attraction was stuck in his eyes. He had a thing for Chase, but Brendan was better looking, in better shape and was more of a disappointment than he was. Chase loved drama and bad boys.

"You are aren't you?" She continued, then burst into mean laughter. "Oh my God, she looks like Shrek!"

Scootie laughed along with us but I could tell he was at a loss for words at Chase's comment. Rather than admit he had to settle for the ugliest bridesmaid he did what every man that has no shot at Chase does.

He succumbed.

"What? You know how many broads I got in my phone I can fuck?" He said, holding his iPhone in a way where his Super

Bowl ring could be visible to Chase and anyone else looking at him.

Damn. Does everyone have an iPhone nowadays?

Suddenly I could feel my own iPhone vibrate inside the front pocket of my black slacks. I had already drowned out Chase's narcissism and Scootie's lovesick puppet act to see Brendan's picture and name flash across the screen.

"Yo?"

"Jeffy, I'm about to stop by the house in about a half. Can you bring Chase? I wanna fuck her one last time before tomorrow."

"What?"

"You know..it's just...." his voice began to trail off as he paused. I could hear soft commotion with a faint sound of generic R&B in the background as his voice slid into a few soft moans. "Hold on..."

Seconds later we were disconnected. I looked at my phone and checked the bars, and they were full, so I knew that the call wasn't dropped.

Now, I wasn't sure what was going on but I knew that whatever it was it had to do with his whorishness. If I'm the unassuming one, and Gene is the black sheep, then Brendan is the Golden Boy of the three Buckley sons. Because he had the good job, the pretty fiancée and had somehow inherited our father's strong jaw line and our mother's *original* beauty. Maybe it was a case of the Middle Child Syndrome in reverse because Gene was a stocky mass of fat and muscle with a stern face and I'm a wiry dude with a baby face. And we're all tall, but other than our height our only saving grace, the thing that our dad said made us stand out from his plainness, was that we all inherited our mother's green doe-eyes. Though for Brendan, he found a way to use his looks to cast a spell on women of all types and invite them to take a ride on his magically delicious Irish dick.

"Who was that?" Chase appeared again. She was like a nosy pixie always popping up out of nowhere.

I gave a nervous laugh, and she saw right through me. Her big brown eyes flickered into disgust for a split second before she immediately turned her attention back to Scootie, who was making his way towards her hideous cousin Whitney. Granted, Whitney had a huge rack and pouty, collagen injected lips of pleasure. Still, the bitch was ugly as sin.

"Come on." Chase grabbed my hand and escorted me past the DJ booth, through the crowd of people uselessly calling out for her a sliver of her attention. In seconds we were both outside in front of the hall in the shivering cold night. I guess wearing a light blue short-sleeve Polo shirt was kinda dumb for the middle of February, but I never thought she would be dragging me outside without a moment to grab my jacket. But the cold didn't affect her as she stood cool as ice, dressed in a form fitting blue Dior suit and sexy heels. The skirt she wore was a little too long for my taste, but it didn't matter because Chase is so stylish. And I know that the beautiful people tend to stick together but damn! Why was she with my dumb ass brother?

"You got a cigarette?" She asked. There was no joy or excitement in her voice. Just a lonely question. Slowly I tore open my pack of Marlboro Lights before she snickered. "You bitch. This is a girl's cigarette."

She wasn't too far from the truth. I had gotten the pack from her cousin Therese. Therese and I dated briefly but I had to stop seeing her after that one time.

Man, I don't even want to get into that again. "Therese smokes these. Did you see her tonight?"

"She was here?" I asked, and Chase laughed because she knew I was full of shit. "She and I came together."

"Guess there's a first time for everything." She joked. Apparently she heard about the time Therese and I had sex and I came within seconds of entering her. But come on now! She was my first.

Actually, she was my first and only. And Therese had been with far more dudes than I had been with girls.

As we stood on the steps smoking in silence I felt my phone vibrate once again. It was a text message from Brendan which simply stated *"Don't bring Chase yet!"*

Whoever he was fucking must have been trash because if he could send a text while he was getting some pussy it must have been a last ditch *I'm About To Get Married* kind of fuck. I laughed to myself as I envisioned Brendan towering over some stupid broad banging her doggy style and texting out of boredom. Suddenly I thought of the time he fucked

that hot Asian girl from his job and texted all of us a picture of his cum littered all over her tits and face after he was done.

Yeah, Brendan's an asshole too.

As I looked up I caught Chase's eyes watching me while she exhaled smoke into the chilly air around us.

"What's up Jeff?" She asked in a tone I wasn't familiar with. "You got a hot date lined up?"

"What? Nah, just a text from one of my boys."

"MmmmHmmm..." She said then took another puff. She tossed the short into the nearby grass and let out a huge sigh. "Let's go. I'm pretty fucked up."

Before I could say anything Chase disappeared into the hall. I shivered as I quickly pulled my phone out again to send Brendan a text, but wasn't able to get it to him before she reappeared with both of our coats.

"You got your truck?" Chase asked as she walked ahead of me. I followed, the two of us making our way to the Ford Explorer my Granddad left me in his will. I took a lot of pride in that car because I loved my Granddad and he left his prized vehicle to me instead of Pop, mainly because they both hated each other and Granddad wanted to give Pop one last *Fuck You Joe!* from beyond the grave. The other two Fuck You's came in the form of the house in Southie he left Gene and the $10,000 he left Brendan.

My mom got an undisclosed figure that she still won't discuss with us but I'm sure she spent it all on plastic surgery, prescription drugs and wine.

Granddad was the original asshole of the family. But he was my buddy, so I let it slide.

"Damn Jeff, you know weed is still illegal right?" Chase said as she got into the passenger seat. I thought that it only *faintly* smelled like weed, but then again I was so used to smoking that I guess I had become immune to the scent.

As we pulled off I noticed Pop outside on the front steps of the hall flagging me down to pull over before we turned out of the parking lot.

"Jeff, your mother's passed out drunk in the coat closet." He said, which made Chase let out a quick laugh. "That's not funny."

"I'm sorry Mr. Buckley." Chase said through a few last chortles while trying to compose herself.

Pop sighed. "No, you're right it is pretty funny. I was hoping I could catch a ride with you-"

"JOSEPH!" a voice screamed from the doors of the hall. It was my Nana Gerri, Mom's mother and Granddad's widow. "I know ya' aren't tryin' ta' *leave* my daughter while she's in this state. Get yer ass back in here and tend to yer wife!"

It was at that moment I realized my dad was trying to leave my mom there to fend for herself with a relative or a neighbor to get home.

Real classy Dad.
But shit, I would have done the same thing.

I *have* done the same thing.

"Christ I hate that old woman." He mumbled before turning around to face his nemesis. "I'm not trying to leave anyone *Gerri*."

"Damn right yer not." Is the last thing I heard before I pulled off. I knew I would hear about this mess when I got home but I couldn't be bothered with them at that moment.

After we crossed the first green light Chase's laughter had finally died down. I honestly didn't think she would ever stop laughing.

"What? That's gonna be *your* family in about sixteen hours."

"No, it's not that..." Chase continued while wiping her eyes. "I love Nana Gerri. She bought me a dildo as a wedding gift. She told me to keep it for those nights when Brendan is outta town." She placed her hand on my resting forearm.

"And she gave me a black one. Then told me it would never be as good as the real thing."

I almost threw up when she told me that. The last thing I needed to know was that some black dude with a huge dick fucked my Nana during Prohibition.

"Come on man." I said, finally letting out a small laugh.

There was a long silence before the two of us noticed that it was beginning to snow. They were small flakes at first but then it started to come down a little heavier.

"I hope it stops soon. I don't want snow on my damn wedding day." Chase said as she leaned forward to look up into the sky through the windshield. "Oooh Jeff look!" I glanced over to see she was pointing at Tadpole Playground. "Remember?"

"Yeah. I haven't been since we were little."

"Pull over." She instructed. I looked at her like she had lost her mind. "Come on, pull over."

"Why?"

"Just pull over Jeff." She said once again, and I obliged. Before the car came to a complete stop she had opened the door and ran out without her jacket. After I parked the car I grabbed her jacket and followed her to see what the hell she was doing.

The heavy snowfall began to blanket everything in front of us with a light coating. I always loved it when it snowed in Boston because it changed the scenery into a living Christmas Card. But shit it was cold. And the little short sleeve shirt I was wearing finally felt like the worse decision I had made of the day.

I followed her over to the old set of swings we used to always spend hours playing on until we all got old enough to realize that the only time boys and girls should really play together is when they're trying to get into each other's pants.

After I caught up to her I could see her taking a photo of the swing set with her phone and then doing something with it, probably uploading it to Instagram.

She began to swipe her finger across the screen, looking at pictures from the night I was assuming and then she stopped for a moment. Her face was frozen as her gaze locked onto one of the pictures for a few seconds, then she gently placed the phone in her skirt pocket.

"Lemme get another cigarette Jeff." She asked. As she took it from the pack I caught a glimpse of her engagement ring once again. Brendan told us he spent a little under five G's on it, but for him that was *Fuck You* money.

He never had any problems with letting us know exactly how much money he made, especially when Scootie was around.

Their Frenemy war had been ongoing for years. When Scootie got drafted to the NFL he bragged about it for months, until Brendan made Junior partner at his law firm and took up the bragging rights by never shutting the fuck up about it. Scootie winning the Super Bowl dug into Brendan's pride for almost a year until he counter-attacked with his news about proposing to Chase. I'm sure Scootie now knew it was his duty to find the perfect trophy wife but if he continued fucking with gargoyles like Whitney Brendan would always be the champion of the *I Got The Baddest Bitch* battle.

The snow was collecting rapidly in Chase's hair as she walked towards and then sat in one of the swings. She looked at me with those pretty brown eyes and patted the swing next to her as an invitation to sit down.

"What's up Chase?"

"Just, come here." She said smiling. And since it was Chase, I obliged.

I know I mentioned that Scootie had a thing for Chase but then again so did most guys that knew her.

Including me.

She's the most beautiful girl I've ever seen. And I've known her long enough to know that her *Girls Gone Wild* persona is just an act.

For the most part.

I mean, she was definitely wild but there were times when it would just be me and her and she would tell me things that she never even told her sisters. Like how when she was sixteen she wanted to become an entomologist and study the life cycles of insects in the Brazilian Rainforest. She had done research and everything.

Still, her mother Miss Connie had been preparing all of her daughters for the high life and when Chase revealed to her the plans she had for college Miss Connie laughed at her and told her that bug chasing was for ugly girls with no future.

I remember Chase cried for days about that.

"God." She said before letting out a sigh that transformed her breath into a huge sequence of steam. "Brendan is so hot."

I chuckled because the statement made me nervous. I've had to deal with girls telling me Brendan was hot, or sexy, or cute as their vague attempt at letting me know I was a permanent resident in their friend zone my entire life. But since she was about to marry him I didn't know what the purpose of her saying this now meant.

"I mean, he's *really* hot." She said again, then took another puff of her cigarette. Then she faced me. "You and Gene never stood a chance."

"Well, Gene's gay so I don't think he stood a chance anyway."

She laughed hard at that.

"I'm sure he gets enough ass." She said, then paused to take another puff. "Or dick."

"Can we not talk about my brother fucking dudes please?" I asked. She countered by leaning over to kiss me.

With tongue.

Her wet smoky mouth tasted like mortal sin. I knew I was supposed to pull away and say something noble like *"What are you doing? You're about to marry my brother"*

But I didn't.

As the two of us slid off of our respective swings onto the cold snowy ground I pictured myself saying *"Chase we can't do this! It's not right. What about Brendan??"* But I couldn't do it.

As I unbuckled my pants and removed her panties I mouthed the word *Stop*! in my head.

Until I entered her.

Her pussy was so warm and wet. And she had such *awesome* control. I buried my head into her neck as she licked my ear and moaned softly. Her hot breath wrapped around my face as I increased speed inside of her. It was so damn good. She trapped me with her legs as an invitation to continue as the snow fell upon us.

I'm not sure how long we fucked but it felt like hours. It was the fulfillment of a fantasy I've had since I was younger and I had no way of stopping myself. Shit, I didn't want to. Even though I knew it was wrong.

As I came I dug my dick deep inside of her, feeling her nails clutch my neck. I raised my head to look into her eyes and she stared at me with an innocence I had never seen in her eyes. I went in to kiss her but she turned away before nudging me to the side so she could get up off the ground. While on my back facing the sky I noticed the snow was stopping. I felt a few light snowflakes caress my dick and fall into my eyes as I caught my breath. By the time I rose to my feet Chase was already peering into her compact mirror to fix her snow covered hair. Her skirt had been lowered and her shirt had been properly smoothed out.

She looked over at me after putting her mirror away and shot me a pitiful smile.

"Hey."

Hey? I thought. ***HEY?!***

"I Love You." I blurted. It echoed amongst the playground for ten seconds before I realized that was probably the wrong thing to say at the time. But it was something I had wanted to say to her for years. Even though I knew she was marrying my brother, I didn't care. I'd always loved her.

And we just fucked! I mean, come on! Wouldn't that be the best time to tell someone you love them?

"Take me to Donna's." She instructed before turning to walk away.

"Wait. You didn't hear what I just said-"

I was interrupted by her phone's 'Baby' by Justin Bieber ringtone. I knew it was Brendan because that was their crappy ass song.

"Hey baby." She answered. "I'm on my way to Donna's now.
Me and Jeff stopped off for another drink."

I couldn't believe her. She was so cold and calculating.

And pretty.

God she's so fucking pretty.
"No, just wait until tomorrow." She continued, then chuckled.
"Stop."

I'm sure he said something nasty to her.

"You're so nasty." she said in a slight sexy growl. "Maybe.
Go to bed baby. Tomorrow."

She hung the phone up as we got into the car. She threw
her head back into the headrest and sighed. "Gimme
another cigarette."

"Um, HELLO" I said. "Did you not hear me when I said *I
Love You* back there?"

"What?" She asked. "Yeah, sure. I love you too Brendan."

"I'm Jeff." I said, and she laughed. "What's so fucking funny?"

"Oh my God. Jeff, don't be so goddamn sensitive." She said as she held out her hand for the cigarette she requested. And since it was Chase, I obliged because I'm a dumb ass.

We drove in silence for about ten minutes until we pulled up to a stop light. Whenever I had the chance I would steal a glance at different parts of her body. My eyes mainly found their resting place at her mouth and her thighs. But the one place I kept looking was at her eyes. Those beautiful eyes that I caught a glimpse of after we had sex. But now, she wouldn't look at me. So I cleared my throat to grab her attention.

"Yes?" She asked, her annoyed eyes rising to the ceiling of the truck.

"What are you doing?"

"Going to Donna's." She replied.

"No" I said. "What are you doing with me?"

"*Going to Donna's.*"

"Gloria." I said. She sighed because only teachers or coworkers ever called her by her first name. "Stop acting dumb. We just fucked. What the fuck are you doing?"

"God Jeff do you think I'm stupid?" She said. "You think I don't know that Brendan is out fucking some other girl right now?"

I remained silent because, honestly, that's probably what everyone thought Brendan was doing when he left the rehearsal dinner so abruptly. Hell, that's probably why Mom was calling him so much. It just never crossed my mind that *Chase* knew.

"Your brother will fuck anything with a hole , and I know this."

She said, finally facing me. "But that's who I'm marrying."

"Do you love him?" I asked. I just had to know before the light changed or before we were dealt any more interruptions. Unfortunately I heard Justin Bieber once more screeching from her skirt pocket, only this time the conversation lasted for the remainder of the ride. When I pulled up in front of Donna's apartment building Chase got out the car giggling on the phone without acknowledging me.

No *See you tomorrow* or *Thanks For The Dick Jeff!*

Nothing.

The car door slamming echoed deep into my soul and her empty laughter sunk into my brain like a tumor as I watched her disappear up the stairs into her pre-nuptial hideout.

There was music on the radio but I couldn't hear it. All I heard was noise. Dull, flat noise that provided a lifeless soundtrack to the bleak background of after midnight Boston in the dead of winter.

In short, quick flashes I was parking the truck, entering the house and plopping down on the couch. It was 12:47 in the morning and I had to somehow muster up the energy to pretend like I didn't just fuck my brother's fiancée hours before their wedding. And on top of that I'm a groomsman so I get the honor of standing up and vouching for both of those assholes.

See how it all comes back to assholes?

I sat on the couch in deep thought until I fell asleep and woke up to arguing coming from the kitchen an hour later.
There were two familiar voices yelling back and forth with an occasional word or two from Mom.

I was slightly hung over so I grabbed my head as I rose to my feet as if doing that would somehow magically make the headache go away. As I entered the kitchen the three of them stopped to look at me.

"What's up Jeffy?" My brother Gene greeted me. "Glad to see you can join us for the bullshit."

"Don't talk like that in front of your mother!" Pop snapped after Mom took a deep gasp like she was offended by Gene's language. "We already discussed why you can't come to the wedding."

"I don't care about *you two*. I'm here to see my little brother get married." Gene stated.

"Well, maybe you can come to the ceremony and sit in the back but leave your gift with one of us and we'll take it to the reception?" Mom suggested. She tried to make it seem like it was her loving way of keeping her son safe from gossip but she was mainly trying to protect *herself* from gossip.

She hated being cast in a light that didn't showcase her as one of the elites of our neighborhood.

"Nice try *Carly*." Gene teased her by using her old Southie nickname *with* the accent. "You're not getting rid of me that easily. It's Brendan's wedding, he invited me and a guest months ago so we'll be at the wedding *and* the reception-"

"A guest?" Pop asked. "What guest?"

"Is it a girl honey?" Mom asked.

And that's when I knew it was about to go from bad to worse so I scooted past the three of them to retrieve the Aleve from the cabinet and a bottle of water from the refrigerator to let them continue their argument in peace.

All my life I have never understood their relationship. They've never spoken to Gene the way they talk to me or Brendan, and he's never talked to them like he was their son.

Maybe it was because they had Gene when they were really young and he was born when they were still living in Southie.

I remember when I was little Gene would always come in whenever he wanted to, talking back to Pop and ignoring

Mom. He never really fit into their new ritzy lifestyle because Gene's presence always represented who they really were regardless of their money and new surroundings.

And after he came out they tried to use that as a reason to keep him from our family but me and Brendan always kept in contact with him. We even knew that he was in a relationship but Gene kept those details very quiet.

"Jeffrey!" Mom peeked her head through my bedroom door. I had the pillow over my head hoping she'd take the hint and leave me alone, but that didn't stop her. "Did you know that Eugene was coming?"

"No Mom." I answered, removing the pillow.

"You think he's lying about Brendan inviting him and his gay lover?" She asked, scurrying from behind the door and closing it. Before I could answer her second question she pulled out that damn sparkly pink phone again. "Brendan it's Mom........No. Who the hell is this *Maude*?" She paused. "OK whatever. Did you invite Eugene to this wedding?"

Her voice scratched at the last bit of sanity I was clinging to, especially after waking up to their argument and still dealing with Chase's icy dismissal.

I could not stop thinking about her. I wondered what she was doing. I imagined her fingering herself in the shower thinking about me. It almost made my dick hard until I remembered Mom was in the room invading my space.

"All right, it's your wedding. But if you want to turn this into an episode of Jerry Springer with ladyboys and whatnot-" she stopped, and I could hear Brendan's voice elevating from the other end of the phone. After a long pause she continued. "Fine. If that's what you want. I can't stop him from coming."

I looked at her to see what she was going to say after she hung the phone up. She sat on the bed next to me and looked at me with loving eyes.

"Jeffrey.....*you* like girls right?"

"God..." I sighed and placed the pillow back over my face.

"I heard about what happened with you and Therese-"

"MOM!" I sprang up.

"I just need to know if you're a gay too. It's not like you have a lot of girls calling here for you-"

"No Mom, I'm not gay." I answered.

She let out a sigh of relief before scooping me into her arms for a hug.

Mom looked at me with a huge grin, tousled my hair and then got up from the bed to check herself in the mirror above my computer desk before she left without another word.

I got out of the bed and locked my bedroom door because I didn't want to see any of them until it was absolutely necessary.

The Wedding

Pop and Gene had been staring at each other from opposite ends of the living room for what seemed like a thousand years. The only sound heard was the loud ticking of the Grandfather clock near the Dining Room, and it got louder as the tension grew. Pop was waiting for Gene's "Guest" to arrive and Gene was waiting for Pop to say something about his "Guest".

Mom was still upstairs getting ready, which really meant she was finishing a bottle of Shiraz and waiting for the Xanax to kick in.

I must've texted Chase a hundred times with stupid nonquestions like *U cool, U Nervous?*, *Can U talk now*?

I figured that her phone was off because she was getting ready for the wedding, but deep down I knew that she was ignoring me.

"I'm ready boys" Mom's voice sang down the stairs as she glided with a sedate grin on her face. As always she was stylish in her cream colored dress and heels. More than likely the dress was Donna Karan and the cost of the shoes equaled someone's monthly mortgage. And of course, she hid her eyes behind dark Chanel shades.

That was a sign that she would be feeling no pain for the next twenty-four hours.

"Great. Now we just gotta wait for the damn limo to get here." Pop said, his eyes still buried deep into Gene's.

"Oh we have a little bit of time then." Mom said before sashaying towards the wine cabinet in the kitchen to open another bottle before any of us could answer. As she hummed a made-up ditty the tension between Pop and Gene was finally cut when Gene let out a painful sigh.

"Joe...." He began. He never called him Pop, always Joe. "The guy who's coming is the guy I've been seeing for the past year."

Pop was silent but his glare became more intense, though Gene never flinched.

He was about to continue his thought but the doorbell ringing interrupted the conversation. The three of us rose to answer the door but Mom, a glass of Shiraz in hand, beat us all to it. There was a guy dressed in an all-black suit and sunglasses standing on the other side.

"Everyone the limo has arrived." She said, then drank the entire glass before continuing. The guy in the doorway looked confused. "It is a later model as I requested is it not?"

"Mrs. Buckley it's me." He said, removing his sunglasses. "Jacob."

"Hello Jacob." She greeted him, her voice never breaking its elitist tone. "You're with the limo company aren't you?"

"Ma..." Gene said after joining her in the doorway. "This is Jake...my *guest.*"

"*Your guest?*" Both Jake and Mom said in unison.

"Hold the fuck up." Pop rose to his feet finally speaking.

"*This* is him?"

"But you're black?" Mom said as she looked Jake up and down repeatedly. "Oh My Lord."

"You never told them about me?" Jake asked.

Mom blurted "He never mentioned you were black-"

"Mom!" I snapped. Before anything else could be said we all noticed a shiny black Lincoln limousine pull up in front of the house. The white limousine driver got out and began walking towards us.

After another round of painful silence and looks of death from Mom to Pop, Pop to Jake and Jake to Gene we all made our way from the front door to the limo. Once inside Mom noticed the complimentary bar in the back of the limo. She reached for a bottle of vodka but Pop restrained her.

There we sat. Mom and Pop facing Gene, Jake and me. Nobody saying a word.

"Seriously." Jake mumbled under his breath then looked over at Gene. "You didn't tell them about me?"

"They knew-"

"Apparently they didn't. Is this why I've never met them?" He asked.

Jake was one hundred percent the type of dude Gene goes for; stocky, masculine and outspoken. I really don't understand why he didn't tell Pop and Mom who he was dating. It's not like they didn't know he was gay, but I guess he knew they'd make a big deal over the fact that Jake is black.

God they suck.

I wish that Gene and Pop would recognize that they're basically the same person but Pop let his homophobia and disappointment always get in the way. And on the flipside Gene let his anti-everything stance and disappointment in our parents get in the way.

"There was never a good time for you all to meet." Gene attempted an excuse, but Jake's face twisted into disapproval. "What?"

"This is some bullshit." Jake said.

"I feel you." Pop blurted out, but that didn't make things any better.

"*I feel you?*" Gene asked. "Is that your attempt at slang?"

"Yeah. Because I've never been around black people before" Pop teased.

"Well there was that one woman Katherine we met a few years ago." Mom said. She then looked over at Jake. "Do you know Katherine?"

"I do." Jake teased. "And she warned me about *you people*."

"Babe" Gene said.

"*Babe?*" Pop asked.

"Lord help us all." Mom said, finally grabbing and opening the bottle of Ketel One to take a huge swig.

As the silence re-entered the limo my phone finally buzzed. It was a text message from Chase:

Stop :/

That was it. Her only words for me after all of those hours of worry and heartache was STOP.

Stop? You ain't say STOP when I was fuckin' you last night!

I wanted to text that back to her sooooo bad. But I couldn't. I wasn't even sure if she would have replied to me if I did.

I didn't even notice the arguing going on around me. It was nothing more than a mess of Pop's resurfacing Southie accent, two angry deep male voices and slurred blurbs from Mom. My heart raced at the thought of finally confronting Chase but everything came to a halt when the limo stopped in front of the church.

"Fuck. We're here." Mom blurted, her accent finally making an appearance.

Now, *Carlene* from Beacon Hill was the pinnacle of class and wealth. *Carly* from Southie, not so much.

So whenever *Carly* made an appearance it wasn't going to be pleasant for anyone.

Pop reached for the door to get out but Mom stopped him.

"OK look. We're here now. You're not about to ruin my baby's day." She then looked over at Pop. "Joe, Jake is here with us so get over it. We're gonna have a good fuckin' time, watch Brendan get married, drink and be fuckin' merry. You got a problem with it, tough. Go the fuck home and sulk on your own time."

Honestly, not only was I shocked, I was happy Carly decided to show up.

"Gene....Shut the fuck up" She got straight to the point with him, then cleared her throat and looked over at Jake.

"Jacob. Have fun. It's an open bar. Chase's family paid for this shit so drink up. And if anyone has something to say to you come get me. I can handle these bitches."

With that she looked at us all, took another swig of the Ketel One, and got out of the car.

There were lots of people milling around on the front steps of the church talking so when Mom got out of the limo all eyes automatically focused on her.

"Hello everyone!" She said, stepping into her ongoing role as the Grand Dame of Beacon Hill once again. "Guess who's here?"

As the rest of us got out of the limo everyone's attention focused on us. Mom immediately walked over and placed her arm around Gene's waist. People's faces turned sour for a moment, but I knew that Mom, now back in Carlene mode, was going somewhere with her performance.

"It's Gene! He's back to see his little brother get married." She squealed, then planted a loving kiss on his cheek. She then looked over at Jake, then back at the crowd watching

us. "Come let's all go inside."

Mom escorted Gene ahead of us but then did something

completely out of character. She grabbed Jake's hand and

pulled him along as me and Pop looked on in awe.

"Is the bar open now?" Pop asked, then looked over at me
before pulling a silver flask out of his suit jacket pocket.

I ignored him and followed Mom into the church. I knew I

had to make my way to the sacristy to meet up with Brendan

and the rest of the groomsmen. As soon as I entered I saw

Scootie, Brendan and his two other groomsmen Donnie and

Hank chugging beer. Scootie finished first of course,

because he's a champion drunk. After he finished his beer

he crushed the can on his head and let out a huge scream.

Brendan and the rest of the guys began slapping high fives

and cheering. Then they all turned to face me.

"JEFF-FAY!!!!" They all screamed as they surrounded me.

Donnie handed me a beer.

"Drink up bitch!" He screamed. And, I tried to finish the whole thing but began gagging almost three quarters of the way through. They all laughed.

"Punk mother fucker!" Hank teased. "You'll never make it through the reception dawg."

Hank was like my third older brother because him and Brendan literally grew up together. When my parents first moved from Southie to Beacon Hill Hank's parents, the Callaghan's, were the first family they met in the neighborhood. They shared a similar story of growing up in a major city. But Mr. and Mrs. Callaghan were both from a neighborhood called Fishtown in Philly. They never spoke much about where they came from either but there was anat understanding between them and my parents that where you came from doesn't dictate where you are right now. And since they never went back to Philly, it resonated with both of my parents because the Callaghan's were also determined to never revisit the past.

Still, as far as Brendan's friends went, Hank was the man. He was cool and down to earth in opposition to Scootie and Donnie's constant yearn of being the biggest asshole in the room. Hank also scored many cool points for marrying his high school sweetheart Natalie a few years ago and the two of them remained the top couple amongst Brendan's friends.

Everyone wanted to marry a girl like Natalie. She was smart, cute in that Girl Next Door kind of way and, surprisingly, not an asshole.

They're the white Barack and Michelle and everyone loves them.

Donnie, on the other hand, was that one friend everyone loved but didn't particularly like. As the shortest of all of them, he had the biggest ego and was a notorious womanizer. And I never understood why since Donnie looked like the bastard spawn of Elmer Fudd and Gonzo.

"Jeffy come outside. Let's smoke." Hank said while Brendan, Donnie and Scootie chugged another beer. We exited through a door leading to a courtyard away from the front entrance. The air was brisk, but the buzz was beginning to kick in so it kept me warm. I waited for Hank to hand me a cigarette as I looked in the opposite direction but when I smelled the familiar scent wafting into my nostrils I recognized exactly what kind of *smoke* he was referring to.

"I can't believe he's marrying that girl." Hank said between puffs. He then handed me the joint. "She's cute, don't get me wrong. But Chase is a hoe."

I chuckled thinking to myself *You have no idea.*

"You think it's a mistake?" I asked.

"Fuck yeah. And I told him too but you know he don't listen to nobody." Hank replied.

"And he still put you in the wedding?" I asked as I handed the joint back to him.

"Because I'm honest. I always been honest with him." He paused to take a hit. "And her. I love Chase but she not marriage material. Not right now at least. She still got crazy daddy issues. I told her to wait but she saw dollar signs and he saw a pretty wife."

Chase lost her father when she was seventeen, right before she went to college. She had always been a Daddy's Girl, and she and Miss Connie didn't have a real solid relationship at the time so the two of them never talked about the problems she was having with the dudes at her school. I remember her calling me on many nights talking about the times guys she slept with would drop her as soon as she revealed that she was falling in love with them. Ironically through all of that drama she kept in contact with Brendan, and eventually their rocky relationship was born. Truth be told when we were growing up Chase hated Brendan. But once his physical appearance changed she was on board with everything. Through their six year off again-on again courtship I think she chose to be with him because she knew he was going to amount to something.

"What are you bitches out here talking about?" Brendan said, his words slurred as he joined us and snatched the joint from Hank's fingertips. "Whisperin' like a bunch of bitches."

"Dude slow down…" Hank said while monitoring the amount of weed Brendan inhaled. "I want you relaxed, not in a damn coma."

"Look, I just wanna get this shit over with so I can take Chase home and finally fuck her in the ass." Brendan said before taking another big hit then coughing hard. A gravelly throat clearing behind us broke our attention as we turned to face Father Riley giving us a look that should have immediately sent us all to hell.

"Gentlemen." His voice cut us to shreds. It was bad enough that the last time we had seen him we were all smoking cigarettes in the back of the rectory.

Smoking weed and talking about anal sex definitely trumps that.

"Hey Father." Brendan greeted him then motioned towards the still lit joint smoldering in his fingers. "You wanna hit?"

Hank let out a nervous laugh then grabbed Brendan to escort him back inside, grabbing the joint and tossing it into the nearby grass before doing so.

I followed behind them, smiling at Father Riley. When I turned the corner I bumped into Chase's cousin Therese and she was the last person I wanted to see.

"Oh…" She greeted me. "Hey Jeff" "Hey

Therese" I said.

"Damn, you couldn't wait until *after* the ceremony?" She asked with her nose scrunched in disgust. It was then I remembered that I still reeked of marijuana.

"Oh, it's not what you think-"

"Therese?" Father Riley's voice interrupted my pathetic excuse. They both hugged for a bit before he smiled and looked her over. "You've grown into quite the pretty young lady."

"Thanks Father." Therese said, her eyes twinkling from the compliment.

His smile disappeared as soon as he looked at me though.

He grunted then walked by me mumbling something in Gaelic.

Therese sighed. "Jeff, did Father Riley catch you smoking weed again?"

"No. It wasn't weed the first time."

She sighed. "That makes it even worse-"

"Brendan was out there with me too."

God this is awkward as hell. The look of disgust and her widened eyes gave way to a slight eye roll before she shook her head and walked off.

"Wait, Therese" I called out. She turned around, deadpan all over her face. "Is Chase here yet?"

"What?" Her expression suddenly changed. "Actually no. That's why I was walkin' around to see if she was hiding somewhere."

"You looked everywhere?"

"Everywhere except the courtyard Snoop." She joked before walking away to return to her mission.

I made my way back to the sanctuary to find Brendan on his knees in front of a trashcan as Hank and Donnie huddled over him. And Scootie, being the asshole that he is, was filming the whole thing with his phone.

"Dude this is gonna get so many hits." He said between demonic laughs "Scootie McBride's Best Friend Earls On His

Wedding Day!"

"Where the hell is your brother?" Pop asked storming over towards me. He pushed me out of the way and stopped short when he noticed Brendan's sad state. "Oh come the fuck on now!"

"Shhhh…." Brendan said, then wiped his mouth. "We're in a church Pop. Don't curse."

"He's completely trashed. How's he gonna get married like this?" Pop asked no one in particular.

After a brief moment of silence Pop noticed that Scootie was still filming.

"Scootie put that phone away or I'm going to ram it up your ass" Pop said, and Scootie wasted no time putting his phone away. He then rushed over to Brendan's side to help Hank and Donnie get him onto his feet. Pop walked over, shaking his head.

"Brendan!" He screamed. At this point he was barely responsive, replying to Pop's yelling with a childish giggle.

"Hank get him some water. Donnie, you stay back here until he sobers up." He then looked at Scootie. "Gimme your phone."

"But Mr. Joe-"

"Gimme your damn phone!" Pop said again, and Scootie sighed while handing the phone over. I wanted to laugh because even after all these years they still respected his authority.

Which I guess is kinda nice in a way, since all of his sons pretty much ignore him.

Pop handed me Scootie's phone. "Jeffrey go out there and stall."

"Uh, Pop-"

"GO!" He screamed, and I went because he clearly was not having a good day and I didn't want to wait around for him to ram Scootie's phone up *my* ass.

When I walked out the church was filled with a continuous sea of whispers and confused faces. Brendan was drunk and Chase was missing. I looked at Mom, sitting in between Jake and Gene, and saw her eyes shoot daggers of despair in my direction. I shrugged my shoulders and felt like a kid again trying to explain to her why I broke her favorite lamp. Her facial expression turned sour as she began to rise but then turned to the aisle at her left as she noticed Miss Connie, long legs and huge rack clad in a low cut pale blue dress, making her way down the aisle.

"Jeffy...." She greeted me in a whisper, her cold eyes accompanying a condescending grin. "Where's your brother?"

"Where's Chase?" I blurted. The flush of panic on her face informed me that she was unaware of Chase's absence.

"Wait here" She whispered before turning to face the guests. "Everyone the wedding will be starting in a few moments. Chase is almost ready."

Miss Connie turned and grabbed my arm to escort me back to the Sanctuary while in the background people began to speak amongst themselves about what the hell was going on.

"Joe." Miss Connie called out, still clutching my arm with a firm grip. "JOE!"

Pop turned around to face Miss Connie. His face said it all.

"Does Carlene know?" He asked.

"No, but I do. Where the hell is Chase?" She asked.

Pop stared at her for a second before responding. "Wait, Chase isn't here?"

"No, your son just asked me where *she* was-" She continued, then stopped mid-sentence when she noticed Brendan sprawled out on the floor as Scootie, Donnie and Hank tried to revive him. "What the hell happened here?"

"He's a little drunk." Pop replied. Miss Connie pushed past Pop and removed Hank from his position as she scooted down next to Brendan and gripped both lapels on his suit jacket.

"Get your ass up Brendan. This wedding ain't cheap!" She said as she shook him.

Pop tried to calm Miss Connie down but her grip and rage were too strong. Scootie and Donnie tried as well, all of their voices escalating to a level that I knew had to be creeping out into the main hall of the church. I was just hoping that Mom didn't hear it.

"Oh my God!" Mom's voice blared from the doorway. She rushed over to the commotion and I stood frozen. I couldn't believe what was going on and then the buzzing from the phone in my front pocket grabbed my attention:

I can't marry him. Not after last night.

It was Chase. I was almost relieved until I realized that I left my phone with Gene and was reading a text from Scootie's phone.

And primarily because Scootie's a complete moron without locks or passwords on his phone I decided to play along since he was preoccupied with Miss Connie beating him across the head with her shoe at the moment:

Last night? Lol

Almost instantly Chase texted back:

Lol asshole. You've gotten much better since last time. I played with my pussy in the shower this morning thinking about you.

THAT BITCH! Hank was right, Chase is a hoe. But then again, so was Brendan so they deserved each other.

I needed to know more.

Where r u?

As the commotion died down around me I never received another text from her. My mind raced through so many different scenarios. I wondered, if she had sex with me before going to her sister's house when did she find the time to have sex with Scootie too? And then it hit me.

What if she changed Scootie's ringtone to Brendan's to throw people off whenever he called her? Because the only person who supposedly called her last night was Brendan.

"All right we need to find Chase." Mom said after Miss Connie was finally calm. "Has anyone spoken to her recently?"

"Not since last night." Scootie said while holding a tissue to the side of his head to stop the bleeding.

"I ain't seen her since the rehearsal yesterday." Brendan, who was finally beginning to make some sense, informed us all. When he said it that's when I knew my theory was right.

"Damn." Gene's voice greeted us all from the doorway.

"You guys really know how to throw a classy wedding."

"What do you want Gene?" Pop asked.

"Jeffy your phone's been blowing up." He said, ignoring Pop and handing me my phone. I had three missed calls from Chase and two text messages. Both of them were similar and cut straight to the point:

At the park. Come now.

"Who is it?" Mom asked.

"Is it Chase?" Miss Connie asked.

"No, it's my friend Dave." I lied. I didn't know anyone named Dave but needed to come up with something quick.

"Just, tell me he's not your boyfriend." Pop said.

"Here we go." Gene started. "You need to get over it Joe-"

"Don't tell me what I need to do-" Pop said. And then another shouting match began, which was perfect because it gave me time to slip away to find a way to get to Chase.

That's when I ran into Therese, again.

"What are you guys doing back here?" She asked, anger plastered all over her face. "People are starting to leave."

"I need to borrow your car-"

"What? The hell with that Bob Marley. You're not wrecking my shit-"

"Chase texted me. She's at the park-"

Her face slid into relief, yet she was still angry. "Why aren't you telling them?"

"Please, let me borrow your car Therese. It's important."

"No" She said. "I'll drive you but you gotta tell me what's going on first."

I wasn't sure if I should tell her the whole truth or just the parts that would make Scootie look bad. Then I remembered that Scootie's an asshole. So I handed his phone over to Therese so she could read the texts.

The ride to the park was very quiet. Therese was still in shock and I didn't want to give up too much information about why I was so involved. The two of us left when Father Riley emerged with two police officers to break up the bickering taking place in the sacristy.

As we approached the park we both noticed the back of a figure in a hoodie and jeans sitting on a swing. No one else was around. I got out of the car and made my way over to her, because I knew it was Chase. I sat down next to her.

She looked over, her eyes wet and red, and smirked. "You've returned to the scene of the crime." She joked, but there was no smile on her face.

"Chase..." I began. I really had no idea what to say to her.

We sat in silence for a moment. I felt awkward and unprepared for a conversation, especially after the way she kept ignoring my attempts to talk to her about last night. Plus I was still mad about her fucking Scootie. I reached into my jacket pocket to pull out a pack of cigarettes and handed it to her, along with my lighter.

She gazed at me then shot her eyes down to the pack and took it.

"I can't marry him." She spoke softly before lighting up. As she blew the smoke out from her mouth she chuckled. "I don't know what the fuck is going on with me Jeffy."

I sighed then looked over my shoulder back to Therese, who was leaning on her car. She cast a look of confusion in my direction with a slight shoulder shrug. I shook my head slightly, hoping she'd leave the situation for me to handle.

"How long have you been out here?" I asked.

"I was driving to the church. Told Donna I wanted some time alone." She paused to take another slow drag. "Then, when I passed by the park I....I don't know." She exhaled. "I started to cry."

"Do you love him?"

Angered she rose from the swing and walked off. I got up and followed her.

"Chase." I called out, grabbing her arm to swing her around. "Do you love him?"

She looked at me, tears in her eyes, then broke away. "No. I don't love *him.*"

We looked at each other without a word to say because her answer was in the silence. The air felt a bit warmer when she said it, and the look in her eyes was filled with conflict and relief. Yet, I still couldn't understand what was going on.

"Dammit Jeff." She said, wiping the tears and composing herself.

I wanted to kiss her but I knew that would only add to Therese's confusion about everything that was going on. Instead I reached into my other pocket and took out

Scootie's phone. I handed it to her and waited for her reaction. Disgust crossed her face before she dropped his phone to the ground and pushed me so hard I fell.

"Chase!" I heard Therese yell, but she ignored it and ran to her car. I sat on the ground motionless as time came to a standstill. Everything moved in slow motion like a movie as I watched Chase get into her car and drive off. I was brought back to reality after I rose to my feet and then felt Therese's hand grab my shoulder.

"What the fuck is going on?" She asked. "What did you say to her?"

Therese looked at me and then noticed Scootie's phone lying on the ground.

I bent down to pick the phone up and placed it back into my pocket. "Let's go."

I didn't wait for her response. It was time to go back to the church and inform everyone that the wedding wouldn't be taking place. Luckily Scootie's phone was only slightly cracked, and I was hoping that he wouldn't notice it.

I sat in Therese's passenger seat smoking a cigarette with the window cracked. I was hoping that the cold air would dissolve the angst I was feeling. On one hand I felt relieved that she loved me, but then there was a part of me that felt terrible for fucking her the night before her wedding. I love my brother. Shit, I love both of my brothers. But how much love could I have for Brendan if I would knowingly fuck his future bride, especially since I was aware of how unstable Chase could be at times. I was hoping the mixture of nicotine and winter chill would somehow inspire me to create a reasonable excuse for why Chase wouldn't be showing up to her own wedding.

During a brief moment of clarity I deleted her messages to Scootie. I knew that with the amount of broads he was fucking he wouldn't miss a few text messages from Chase.

At least that's what I was hoping for.

Therese was quiet during the ride back but her mouth finally parted to speak when we drove up and saw Chase's car neatly parked in the driveway.

"Man, that girl is a mess." She said before opening the door. "You gonna tell them about the park?"

With no more emotion left to give I looked at her with somber eyes. "For what?"

I got out of the car and walked away, somewhat happy that Chase didn't ditch my brother at the altar. Still I knew that if she chose to marry Brendan what she told me moments ago meant nothing anymore.

Mom made her way over to me as soon as I entered the church.

"Jeffrey where the hell-" She stopped then looked around. "Shit, we're in a church. I shouldn't be cursing."

"What's up Mom? Everything good?"

"Oh, yes." She said, now facing me. "Chase went to the cemetery to see her father. Said she got nervous and wanted to talk to him."

"Really?" I asked, sarcastic grin in place but I knew she wouldn't pick up on it. "What about the cops?"

"Oh that little thing? They arrested Gene."

"What?! Why?"

"Carlene" Miss Connie interrupted us. "Chase is almost ready. Donna and Christy are finishing her make-up."

"Good. She looked awful when she got in." Mom quipped. "You have any more wine?"

The two of them made their exit back down the aisle as guests watched them, chattering just above a whisper. Many guests had left but more than half chose to wait around as our family drama unfolded. I looked through the crowd for Jake but I couldn't locate him. I assumed that he went with Gene as he was carted to the police station.

"Mom." I called out before she could get too far from my reach to hand her Scootie's phone. "Give this to Scootie. Tell him it slipped outta my pocket when I left earlier."

Mom smirked. "Oh that won't bother him. He's got money."

"Let me know when you're ready for me." I said as she continued back towards the sacristy with Miss Connie.

The Reception

I must have been two Jack and Ginger's in by the time the appetizer was served. Throughout the night I found myself looking over in Chase and Brendan's direction at their table in the center of the reception hall near the dance floor laughing and kissing. One more Jack and Ginger in and I saw them kissing well-wishers and hugging close friends. Scootie stood with Hank, Natalie and his parents at the bar while Joe and Carlene floated together through the room conversing with various people.

And none of it seemed real.

Actually, all of it seemed like a dream to me. Two more Jack and Ginger's in, after the main course was served Miss Connie did the traditional Father-Daughter dance with Chase, causing tears and applause from everyone in the room.

"Connie raised those girls all by herself after Phillip died." I overheard one guest say.

As the night wore on every guest who bought into the fantasy of this madness relayed their personal reviews of the whole day.

"Those girls are all Connie have now."

"God Chase is almost as beautiful as Connie was back then. Remember her and Phillip?"

"Phil is smiling on all of his girls right now."

"Brendan only has eyes for Chase."

"They'll never have to worry about money."

"Is this an open bar?"

"Joe and Carlene sure raised a fine young man."

"Who was that black guy earlier?"

"Joe's gay son got arrested for hitting him earlier."

"Scootie has always had Brendan's back!"

I never tried to correct anyone who didn't know what was really going on. I barely spoke the entire evening while observing the same thing I had the night before at the rehearsal dinner.

It was all bullshit.

My family. Their friends. This marriage. All of it was bullshit. I damn near threw up whenever I saw Scootie and Chase hug because I was the only one who knew what was going on.

Then, through Lady GaGa's *Poker Face* I heard Pop's voice cut into the music.

"Excuse me everyone." He commanded their attention through a handheld microphone with his bellowing voice. The DJ took her cue to lower the music so everyone would give Pop their full attention. "I want to say something."

Joe Buckley knew how to talk to people when it was necessary. I had a lot of gripes about Pop but the one thing I could say about him is that he was well respected in our community. Most people that knew him liked him. They loved his story of removing himself from Southie to become a man of distinction and wealth, which was a characteristic that I can honestly say I love about my father.

But sometimes, I didn't necessarily *like* him.

"Brendan.." He started after everyone was listening. "Man, you make me so very proud. I always knew I was going to stand here one day at you and Chase's wedding and I always knew what I wanted to say. But now, I can't find the words." He stopped, then looked around the room. "Imagine *me*. Speechless."

People laughed at his joke which made him smile. He continued. "No seriously. I love you Brendan. Your mother and I have worked very damn hard to make sure you and your brother never had to worry about anything. I knew when you were born that I needed to invest my all in you and I'm so glad to be here to watch you marry the most beautiful girl in Boston."

That garnered applause and hollers from the room. My mother even raised her glass towards the two of them showing everyone her sparkling veneers.

He then raised his glass. "A toast. To Mr. and Mrs. Brendan Buckley." He then looked over at Chase. "You're one of us now darlin'. You've been warned."

Everyone laughed at that remark then my father concluded the toast with a *Slainte*.

The DJ brought the music back up into Kool and the Gang's *Celebration*. But I wasn't in any mood to pretend like I wanted to celebrate.

"I GOT SOMETHING TO SAY!" I shouted as I rose from my table, only to hit my knee against it and knock everything to the ground. Clearly I got everyone's attention, but mostly they all laughed at my drunken state.

"Chase, I warned you." Pop spoke into the mic, getting one last laugh from the guests as the caterers came over to clean up my mess. I guess after my last two Jack and

Gingers I really was in no condition to speak my piece.
I tried to help them clean up, but they wouldn't let me. When I felt someone helping me to my feet and whisking me outside of the reception area I had no idea what was going on.

It was Therese. She sat me down in a chair and handed me a mug of hot coffee.

"Jeff." She said, sitting in the seat next to me. "Hey."

I was a little fucked up but not to the point where I couldn't focus. "Hey Reecie."

She chuckled. "You're drunk."

"Nah...." I took a sip before continuing. "I'm awake."

"Really?"

"Yeah. I'm awake." I took another sip then started laughing. "To the bullshit!"

I laughed uncontrollably for a few minutes, feeling the death glares I was getting from people nearby.

Then I stopped laughing. "Yo, did you hear him?" I paused. "*You and your brother.*"

She sighed. "I noticed that."

"Pop is an asshole."

"Everyone knows that." She said with a chuckle. "But, what are you gonna do?"

"I'm going to expose them all." I slurred.

"Oh, now you're Diane Sawyer?" She said. "You're gonna go to your parents and say what exactly?"

I couldn't think of anything that I would be able to say to them that wouldn't come off as the ranting of a belligerent drunk. I looked back into the reception hall and saw Mom, Pop, Chase and Brendan gather together for a picture.

"Come on." She said, holding my hand and leading me outside. I was surprised to see Jake leaning against a taxicab in the parking lot. I looked over at Therese and she smiled at me, which was something she never did, and then went back inside to leave me with him.

"Hey Jeff." He greeted me. "You OK?"

"Yeah man, I'm good." I answered, shaking his hand. "Are you coming in?"

He laughed. "Hell no. I don't do drama."

"How's Gene?"

Jake's eyes widened. "How do you think? He got into a fist fight with your dad and then got arrested."

"Where is he-"

"He's cool, he's cool." Jake said. "NaNa Gerri bailed him out after your father dropped the charges."

That's when I noticed that Gene was in the cab looking out from the window. Jake moved out of the way and opened the door for me to get inside.

"Hey Jeffy." He said after I got in. "How was it?"

"Bullshit." I answered, and he chuckled. "You OK?"
Gene was too cool as he shrugged the whole situation off.

"What, *this*? Please, this ain't the first time me and *your father* fought."

"Are you gonna come in?"

"Fuck no." He stated. "I'll catch them later."

He reached into his pocket and handed me an envelope.

"Give that to Chase and tell her I'm sorry we missed her before our flight to Raleigh."

"Raleigh?"

Gene looked at me, smiling with sadness in his eyes. "I'm leaving Jeff. Me and Jake found gigs and a house down there."

God could this fuckin' day get any worse?

"I mainly came today to see Brendan get married, but we were always leaving tonight."

"Does Brendan know?" I asked and he nodded. "Well why didn't you tell me?"

"I don't know man. It was hard enough telling Brendan..." He paused then sighed. "Just, promise me you won't become like them man."

"You make it seem like you're never coming back."

"I'm not. This ain't my home." He looked past me noticing Mom standing in the entrance of the hall. "It wasn't always like this bro. I love them but I can't be around them. They bring out the worse in me."

I wasn't sure if it was the stress of the entire day or the alcohol but knowing that he was leaving for good was the trigger for tears to start falling from my eyes. Gene reached over and hugged me, patting my back to soothe my cries.

"Stop crying Jeffy. I'ma always be here for you." He said then pulled away. "You've got a home in Raleigh whenever you need it, OK?"

I nodded my head and forced a smile. I was really going to miss him.

I got out of the taxi, shook Jake's hand and stood in the parking lot as I watched the taxi drive off into the night.
Suddenly Mom was standing beside me.

"Jeffrey.." She said. I didn't want to talk to her at that moment but she was persistent. "Honey look at me."

I was hesitant but I turned to face her. "He's leaving Mom."

"It's for the best Jeffy." She said, her eyes giving way to a small amount of regret. "I love Eugene-"

"Whatever" I said then turned to go back inside. But she followed me and stopped me at the door.

"Jeffrey I love all of you. But I cannot afford to have him living here if he chooses to be into that kind of lifestyle-" "But he's your son Mom!" I screamed. "Did you forget?"

"He's been *my son* since I was sixteen." She replied, then stopped before becoming too emotional or loud. "I was the one who convinced your father to drop the charges."

"It's fucked up Mom."
"No, it's life Jeff. This is our lives. This is our family." She then lowered her voice to just above a whisper. "She's Brendan's wife now. His *wife*. Do you understand?"

I wasn't sure what she was alluding to at first but it didn't take long before I caught on.

"You know about me and Chase?"

She let out a quick laugh before her face turned stern. "No. I don't know anything. And neither do you. Understand?"

Once again it began to snow, big fat flakes that hit the ground and covered everything in a light coating.

"Come inside soon honey." She said, straightening out my suit jacket and then placing a kiss on my right cheek. "They're about to cut the cake."

Mom left me outside to collect my thoughts. I watched the snow accumulate; blanketing everything it touched in a soft sea of white. I pulled a cigarette out and smoked as I watched God's dandruff, as Granddad used to call it, dance in the air in a symphony of beauty. I said a silent prayer for Gene and Jake's flight, flicked my cigarette to the ground once I was finished and returned inside to witness my family continue the charade they

called life.

<u>One Year Anniversary Dinner</u>

My flight left Dulles on time, but it was rocky as hell. Honestly I thought that the plane was going to drop out of the sky when the snowstorm hit right before we touched down in Boston. I was armed with toys for little Brendan that I got from Gene and Jake, which worked perfectly since I was broke as hell and couldn't afford anything.

Mom told me that I could stay with her and Pop while I was in town but I opted for a hotel near the airport and a rental so I could do the family thing and get the hell outta there by morning.

When I got to the restaurant everyone burst into happy greetings once they saw me. Brendan hugged me so hard I thought I was going to shit out a lung. Chase followed suit by hugging me, but it was light and quick.

Scootie was back home in New York but sent his gifts with his parents. All of the usual suspects were there, including Therese, who was now expecting her first kid with Donnie, of all people.

Mom and Miss Connie must have guzzled down about six bottles of wine between the both of them and Pop was being his normal charming self, cursing out a bartender who cut him off after one too many Glenlivet's.

Chase and I barely spoke anymore. After I graduated last spring and moved to DC the only time I ever spoke to her was on Facebook, and Brendan was so busy with his law firm he and I could only find time to talk once or twice a month. But he always told me how proud he was of me for having the balls to leave Boston and live on my own so far away from everything I knew.

He had no idea that for me there was no other option.

Before I left to go back to my hotel I hugged and kissed everyone. Pop slipped a hundred dollar bill in my pocket and told me he loved me. Mom retrieved the hundred when she hugged me and whispered "Don't tell your father"

Classic Carly I thought to myself. Brendan, who was pretty bombed by the end of the night, wouldn't stop hugging me before he and Chase got into their cab to go home.

"Good to see you Jeffy." Chase said as we hugged, she then pulled away. "Oh wait. I have something for you."

She dug into her clutch and pulled out an envelope. Inside was a picture of Little Brendan. Hate to admit it but he's a cute little fucker. Still, he wasn't cute enough for me to want to have a kid now. I was having too much fun with the

Nightlife and ladies of DC.

"Wow. He looks just like us." I said, grinning from ear to ear.

Chase laughed. "No. He looks just like his father."

I chuckled, but when I realized her silence the look in her eyes revealed the true story.

And once again I was back where I left off with her.

ABOUT THE AUTHOR

Since the age of sixteen Ben Robinson III has been writing poetry, plays and novels with the dream of one day becoming a published author. *The Buckleys*, a story that originated from a prompt during a writer's workshop, is his first published story and the achievement of a lifelong dream finally coming to fruition.

Made in the USA
Middletown, DE
02 July 2021